Little Songs of Long Ago

A COLLECTION OF FAVORITE POEMS AND RHYMES

Illustrated by

HENRIETTE WILLEBEEK LE MAIR

PHILOMEL BOOKS

New York

A NOTE ABOUT THE ORIGINAL BOOK

First published in England in 1912, when Henriette Willebeek le Mair was twenty-three, *Little Songs Of Long Ago* was her fifth book and along with its companion, *Our Old Nursery Rhymes*, established le Mair's international reputation. The original book contained musical arrangements and slight differences in artwork and design, but its feeling and content was very much like the book we publish today.

Contents

Curly locks, Curly locks,
  Wilt thou be mine?
Thou shalt not wash dishes
  Nor yet feed the swine;
But sit on a cushion
  And sew a fine seam,
And feed upon strawberries,
  Sugar and cream.

Hickory, Dickory, Dock

Hickory, dickory, dock,
The mouse ran up the clock;
The clock struck one,
The mouse ran down,
Hickory, dickory, dock.

Dickery, dickery, dare,
The pig flew up in the air;
The man in brown
Soon brought him down,
Dickery, dickery, dare.

Dame, Get Up And Bake Your Pies

Dame, get up and bake your pies,
  Bake your pies, bake your pies;
Dame, get up and bake your pies,
    On Christmas day in the morning.

Dame, what makes your maidens lie,
    Maidens lie, maidens lie;
Dame, what makes your maidens lie,
    On Christmas day in the morning?

Dame, what makes your ducks to die,
    Ducks to die, ducks to die;
Dame, what makes your ducks to die,
    On Christmas day in the morning?

Three little mice sat down to spin;
Pussy passed by and she peeped in.
What are you doing, my little men?
    Weaving coats for gentlemen.
Shall I come in and cut off your threads?
    No, no, Mistress Pussy, you'd bite off our heads.
Oh, no, I'll not; I'll help you to spin.
    That may be so, but you don't come in.

*H*ere am I,
　Little Jumping Joan;
When nobody's with me
　I'm all alone.

Little Polly Flinders
Sat among the cinders,
Warming her pretty little toes;
Her mother came and caught her,
And whipped her little daughter
For spoiling her nice new clothes.

Pat-a-Cake

Pat-a-cake, pat-a-cake, baker's man,
Bake me a cake as fast as you can;
Pat it and prick it, and mark it with B,
Put it in the oven for baby and me.

London Bridge Is Falling Down

London Bridge is falling down,
    Falling down, falling down,
London Bridge is falling down,
    My fair lady.

Build it up with wood and clay,
    Wood and clay, wood and clay,
Build it up with wood and clay,
    My fair lady.

Wood and clay will wash away,
    Wash away, wash away,
Wood and clay will wash away,
    My fair lady.

Built it up with silver and gold,
    Silver and gold, silver and gold,
Build it up with silver and gold,
    My fair lady.

Silver and gold will be stolen away,
    Stolen away, stolen away,
Silver and gold will be stolen away,
    My fair lady.

Set a man to watch all night,
    Watch all night, watch all night,
Set a man to watch all night,
    My fair lady.

*L*ittle Tommy Tucker
  Sings for his supper:
What shall we give him?
    White bread and butter.
How shall he cut it
    Without e'er a knife?
How will he be married
    Without e'er a wife?

Where Are You Going To?

Where are you going to, my pretty maid?
  I'm going a-milking, sir, she said,
Sir, she said, sir, she said,
  I'm going a-milking, sir, she said.

May I go with you, my pretty maid?
  You're kindly welcome, sir, she said,
Sir, she said, sir, she said,
  You're kindly welcome, sir, she said.

Say, will you marry me, my pretty maid?
  Yes, if you please, kind sir, she said,
Sir, she said, sir, she said,
  Yes, if you please, kind sir, she said.

What is your father, my pretty maid?
  My father's a farmer, sir, she said,
Sir, she said, sir, she said,
  My father's a farmer, sir, she said.

What is your fortune, my pretty maid?
  My face is my fortune, sir, she said,
Sir, she said, sir, she said,
  My face is my fortune, sir, she said.

Then I can't marry you, my pretty maid.
  Nobody asked you, sir, she said,
Sir, she said, sir, she said,
  Nobody asked you, sir, she said.

Sing a song of sixpence,
A pocket full of rye;
Four and twenty blackbirds,
Baked in a pie.

When the pie was opened,
The birds began to sing;
Was not that a dainty dish,
To set before a king?

The king was in his counting-house,
Counting out his money;
The queen was in the parlour,
Eating bread and honey.

The maid was in the garden,
Hanging out the clothes,
When down came a blackbird,
And pecked off her nose.

Oranges and Lemons

Oranges and lemons,
Say the bells of St. Clement's.

You owe me five farthings,
Say the bells of St. Martin's.

When will you pay me?
Say the bells of Old Bailey.

When I grow rich,
Say the bells of Shoreditch.

When will that be?
Say the bells of Stepney.

I do not know,
Says the great bell at Bow.

Simple Simon met a pieman
Going to the fair;
Says Simple Simon to the pieman,
Let me taste your ware.

Says the pieman to Simple Simon,
Show me first your penny;
Says Simple Simon to the pieman,
Indeed I have not any.

Simple Simon went a-fishing,
For to catch a whale;
All the water he had got
Was in his mother's pail.

Simple Simon went to look
If plums grew on a thistle;
He pricked his finger very much,
Which made poor Simon whistle.

He went to catch a dickey bird,
And thought he could not fail,
Because he'd got a little salt,
To put upon its tail.

He went for water in a sieve,
But soon it all ran through;
And now poor Simple Simon
Bids you all adieu.

Lavender's Blue

*L*avender's blue, dilly, dilly,
  Lavender's green;
When I am king, dilly, dilly,
    You shall be queen.

Call up your men, dilly, dilly,
    Set them to work,
Some to the plough, dilly, dilly,
    Some to the cart.

Some to make hay, dilly, dilly,
    Some to thresh corn,
Whilst you and I, dilly, dilly,
    Keep ourselves warm.

Old King Cole

Old King Cole
Was a merry old soul,
And a merry old soul was he;
    He called for his pipe,
And he called for his bowl,
And he called for his fiddlers three.

Every fiddler he had a fiddle,
    And a very fine fiddle had he;
Twee tweedle dee, tweedle dee, went the fiddlers.
    Oh, there's none so rare
As can compare
With King Cole and his fiddlers three.

A Frog He Would A-Wooing Go

A frog he would a wooing go
  "Heigh-ho!" said Rowley;
Whether his mother would
let him or no,
    With a rowly powly,
    Gammon and spinach,
"Heigh-ho!" said Anthony Rowley.

Off he set with his opera hat,
    "Heigh-ho!" said Rowley;
Off he set with his opera hat,
And on the road he met with a rat,
    With a rowly powly,
    Gammon and spinach,
"Heigh-ho!" said Anthony Rowley.

So they arrived at the mouse's hall,
    "Heigh-ho!" said Rowley;
They gave a loud tap,
and they gave a loud call,
    With a rowly powly,
    Gammon and spinach,
"Heigh-ho!" said Anthony Rowley.

"Pray, Mr. Frog, will you give us a song?"
    "Heigh-ho!" said Rowley;
"Let the subject be something
that's not over long,"
    With a rowly powly,
    Gammon and spinach,
"Heigh-ho!" said Anthony Rowley.

"Indeed, Mrs. Mouse!" replied the frog,
    "Heigh-ho!" said Rowley;
"A cold has made me
as hoarse as a hog,"
    With a rowly powly,
    Gammon and spinach,
"Heigh-ho!" said Anthony Rowley.

"Since you have caught a cold,
Mr. Frog," mousy said,
    "Heigh-ho!" said Rowley;
"I'll sing you a song that I have just made,"
    With a rowly powly,
    Gammon and spinach,
"Heigh-ho!" said Anthony Rowley.

Boys and Girls, Come Out to Play

Boys and girls, come out to play,
The moon doth shine as bright as day.
Leave your supper and leave your sleep,
    And join your playfellows in the street.
Come with a whoop and come with a call,
    Come with a good will or not at all.
Up the ladder and down the wall,
    A half-penny loaf will serve us all;
You find milk, and I'll find flour,
    And we'll have a pudding in half an hour.

Seesaw, Margery Daw

Seesaw, Margery Daw,
Jacky shall have a new master;
Jacky shall have but a penny a day,
Because he can't work any faster.

Tom, he was a piper's son,
    He learnt to play when he was young,
And all the tune that he could play,
    Was, "Over the hills and far away";
Over the hills and a great way off,
    The wind shall blow my top-knot off.

Tom with his pipe made such a noise,
    That he pleased both the girls and boys,
And they all stopped to hear him play,
    "Over the hills and far away."
Over the hills and a great way off,
    The wind shall blow my top-knot off.

I Had a Little Nut Tree

I had a little nut tree,
    Nothing would it bear
But a silver nutmeg
    And a golden pear;
The king of Spain's daughter
    Came to visit me;
And all because of my little nut tree.

The Babes in the Wood

My dear, do you know,
How a long time ago,
Two little children, whose names I don't know,
Were stolen away
On a fine summer's day,
And left in a wood, as I've heard people say.
    Poor babes in the wood!
    Poor babes in the wood!
And don't you remember the babes in the wood?

And when it was night,
So sad was their plight,
The sun it went down, and the moon gave no light!
They sobb'd and they sigh'd,
And they bitterly cried,
And the poor little things, they then lay down and died.
    Poor babes in the wood!
    Poor babes in the wood!
And don't you remember the babes in the wood?

And when they were dead,
The robin so red
Brought strawberry leaves and over them spread;
And all the day long,
The branches among,
They sang them this song,
    "Poor babes in the wood!
    Poor babes in the wood!
Don't you remember the babes in the wood?"

Twinkle, Twinkle, Little Star

Twinkle, twinkle, little star,
How I wonder what you are!
Up above the world so high,
Like a diamond in the sky.

When the blazing sun is gone,
When he nothing shines upon,
Then you show your little light,
Twinkle, twinkle, all the night.

In the dark blue sky you keep,
And often through my curtains peep,
For you never shut your eye,
Till the sun is in the sky.

As your bright and tiny spark,
Lights the traveller in the dark,
Though I know not what you are,
Twinkle, twinkle, little star.

When the traveller in the dark,
Thanks you for your tiny spark,
He could not see which way to go,
If you did not twinkle so.

Lazy sheep, pray tell me why
  In the pleasant field you lie,
Eating grass and daisies white
    From the morning 'till the night?
Ev'rything can something do,
    But what kind of use are you?

"Nay, my little master, nay
    Do not serve me so, I pray;
Don't you see the wool that grows
    On my back to make your clothes?
Cold, ah, very cold you'd be
    If you had not wool from me."

I Saw Three Ships

I saw three ships come sailing by,
  Come sailing by, come sailing by,
I saw three ships come sailing by,
  On New-Year's day in the morning.

And what do you think was in them then,
  Was in them then, was in them then?
And what do you think was in them then,
  On New-Year's day in the morning?

Three pretty girls were in them then,
  Were in them then, were in them then,
Three pretty girls were in them then,
  On New-Year's day in the morning.

One could whistle, and one could sing,
  And one could play the violin;
Such joy there was at my wedding,
  On New-Year's day in the morning.

The Crooked Man

There was a crooked man,
     and he walked a crooked mile,
He found a crooked sixpence
     Against a crooked stile;
He bought a crooked cat,
     Which caught a crooked mouse,
And they all lived together
     In a little crooked house.

Four and twenty tailors
   Went to kill a snail,
The best man among them
   Durst not touch her tail;
She put out her horns
   Like a little Kyloe cow,
Run, tailors, run,
   Or she'll kill you all e'en now.

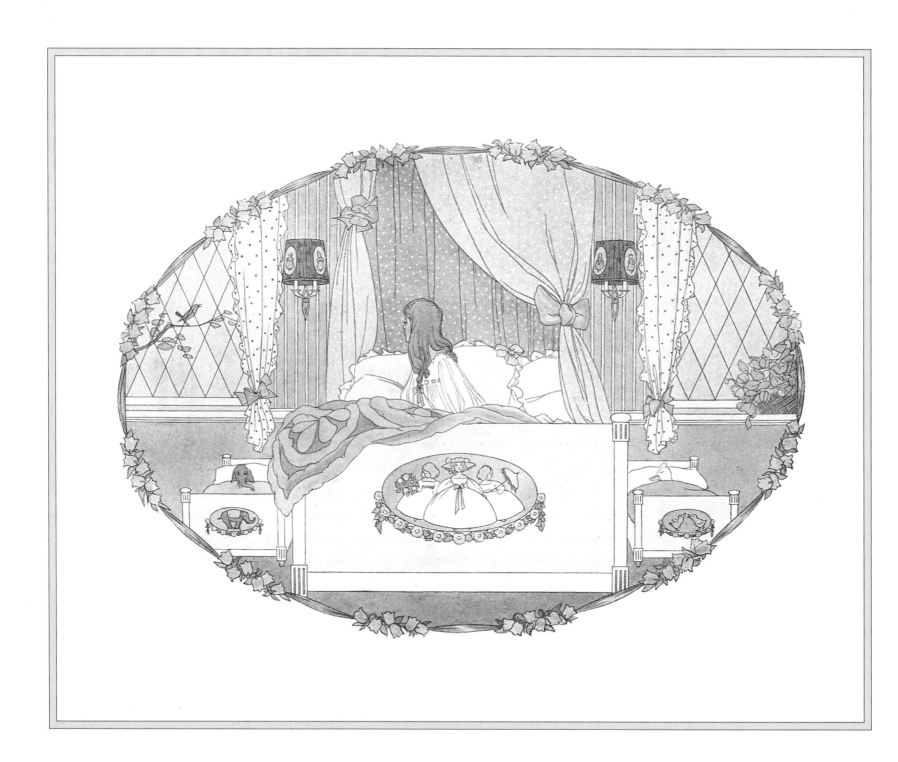

There Came to My Window

There came to my window one morning in spring
A sweet little robin, she came there to sing;
The tune that she sang it was prettier far
Than any I heard on the flute or guitar.

Her wings she was spreading to soar far away,
Then resting a moment seem'd sweetly to say —
"Oh happy, how happy the world seems to be,
Awake, little girl, and be happy with me!"

The Spider and the Fly

"Will you walk into my parlour?" said the spider to the fly —
"'Tis the prettiest little parlour that ever you did spy.
The way into my parlour is up a winding stair;
    And I have many curious things to show you when you're there."
"Oh, no, no," said the little fly; "To ask me is in vain;
    For who goes up your winding stair can ne'er come down again."

The spider turned him round about, and went into his den,
    For well he knew the silly fly would soon come back again,
So he wove a subtle web in a little corner sly,
    And set his table ready, to dine upon the fly.
Then he came out to his door again, and merrily did sing —
    "Come hither, hither, pretty fly, with the pearl and silver wing."

Alas! Alas! how very soon this silly little fly,
    Hearing his wily flattering words, came slowly flitting by.
With buzzing wings she hung aloft, then near and nearer drew;
    Thinking only of her brilliant eyes, her green, gold and purple hue.
Thinking only of her crested head — poor silly thing! At last,
    Up jumped the cunning spider, and firmly held her fast!

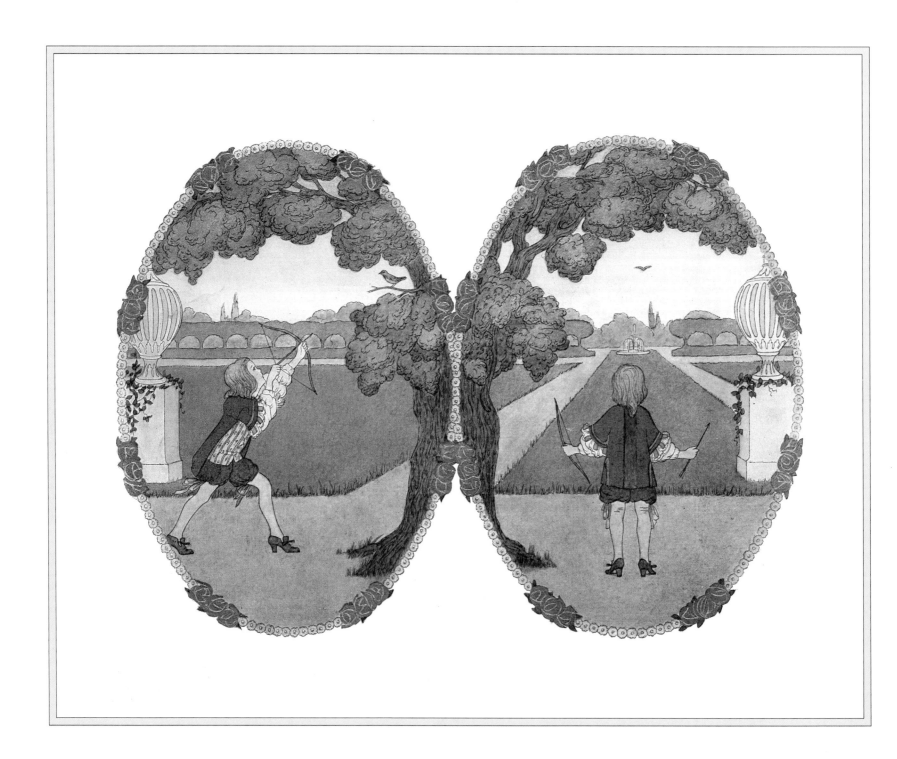

A little cock sparrow sat on a green tree,
    And he chirruped, he chirruped, so merry was he.
A naughty boy came with his wee bow and arrow,
    Says he, I will shoot this little cock sparrow;
His body will make me a nice little stew,
    And his giblets will make me a little pie too.
Oh, no, said the sparrow, I won't make a stew,
    So he clapped his wings and away he flew.

Sleep, Baby, Sleep

Sleep, baby, sleep,
 Our cottage vale is deep;
The little lamb is on the green,
 With woolly fleece so soft and clean —
Sleep, baby, sleep.

Sleep, baby, sleep,
 Thy rest shall angels keep:
While on the grass the lamb shall feed,
 And never suffer want or need.
Sleep, baby, sleep.

Sleep, baby, sleep,
 Down where the woodbines creep;
Be always like the lamb so mild,
 A kind, and sweet, and gentle child.
Sleep, baby, sleep.

INDEX OF FIRST LINES